I FOUND A KITTY!

DEAR DIARY, **WOOF!** TODAY I PLAYED OUTSIDE.

IT WAS TUESDAY, SO I DUG UP A STICK AND BARKED AT A BIRD.... BUT THEN I SMELLED SOMETHING NEW.

IT WAS A FRIEND!

HE NEEDED A HOME, SO I GOT TO WORK.

I FOUND A KITTY!

TROY CUMMINGS

SCHOLASTIC INC.

DEAR MUSIC TEACHER,

I FOUND A KITTY! CAN YOU HELP HIM?

HIS NAME IS SCAMPER!

I REALLY REALLY REALLY WANT TO KEEP HIM, BUT MY PERSON IS ALLERGIC TO CATS.

SCAMPER LIKES TO EAT, PLAY, AND POOP IN A BOX. HE ALSO LIKES TO SING! I KNOW HE WOULD MAKE ♪ BEAUTIFUL MUSIC ♫ WITH YOUR STUDENTS.

YOUR NEIGHBOR,

ARFY

Dear Arfy,

Scamper is a wonderful kitten. His tail twitches to the beat!

But his high notes are simply too much.

I'm sorry. I was hoping for more harmony in my household. But with Scamper here, I can hardly find a single measure of rest.

Best wishes in your search,

Maestro Mitch

DEAR CUTE LITTLE
NEIGHBOR BABIES,

I FOUND A KITTY!

HE'S A LOT LIKE YOU. HE TAKES
NAPS, EATS EVERY TWO HOURS,
AND LIKES TO CRAWL UNDER
THE COUCH ON HIS TUMMY.

CAN YOU HELP HIM?

SINCERELY,
ARFY

Dear Arfy,

We have wanted a widdle itty-bitty kitty since the day we were born!

We snuggled with him in the morning, nuzzled with him in the afternoon, and squeezed him like a teddy bear at night.

But then a funny thing happened. He squirmed out of our arms and ran out the door.

Guess we'll go back to snuggling our fuzzy-wuzzy sheep blankie.

Bennie, Bonny, and Boo

DEAR NICE MECHANIC,

CAN YOU HELP MY KITTY?

I SAW A MOUSE AT YOUR GARAGE
ONE TIME, AND WE ALL KNOW
CATS ARE GREAT AT CHASING MICE!

I'LL BET SCAMPER WOULD POUNCE
ON THE CHANCE TO HELP YOU OUT.

YOUR PAL,
ARFY

LUGNUT GARAGE

Dear Arfy,

You're right. My garage has a HUGE mouse problem. Those little squeakers are bumper-to-bumper in here!

I was all revved up to give Scamper a chance. But he didn't eat a single mouse—he just played with them!

Sorry to throw a wrench in your plans, but I need a mouser who's willing to sink his teeth into his work.

Emily Lugnut
Mechanic

Thank You!

TO THE PEOPLE IN THE FANCY BUILDING
WITH THE RED CARPET OUT FRONT,

CAN YOU HELP MY KITTY?

SCAMPER'S FUR IS SHINY,
AND HIS EYES
ARE SPARKLY - LIKE THE
STARS ON YOUR SIDEWALK.

WOOF ALL DUE RESPECT,

ARFY

TELEGRAM

TO Arfy   **FROM** Melissa Glitz, talent agent

Arfy, baby!

I've been on the prowl for someone like Scamper. From the moment he entered my studio, I knew he'd be a superstar.

All I had to do was style his fur. And polish his teeth. And do something about those claws.

But then, right after his photo shoot, Scamper gagged. And twitched. And hacked up a two-pound hair ball. Right into my designer handbag.

So sorry, darling, but our little glamorpuss would be more at home on a living room rug than on the red carpet.

xoxo

Missy

DEAR CAT-LOVER GUY,

I WAS SNIFFING AROUND YOUR BUSHES, AND I NOTICED SOMETHING ABOUT YOUR HOUSE,

YOU HAVE CAT CURTAINS, A CAT CLOCK, CAT WALLPAPER, A CAT SOFA, A CAT TOILET SEAT, AND A WHOLE BUNCH OF TINY SHINY CAT STATUES.

BUT YOU DON'T HAVE AN ACTUAL CAT!

CAN YOU HELP MY KITTY? I THINK SCAMPER WOULD FIT RIGHT IN.

HOPEFULLY,
ARFY

Dear Arfy,

I've spent my whole life collecting kitty-cat knickknacks. Scamper is just what I was missing!

Our first morning together was dreamy. I fed him, brushed him, and tucked him in to his kitty bed. We both purred with delight.

But then he started to play. That frisky kitten knocked over my entire collection of ceramic cats! My figurines—and my heart—were shattered.

I'm sorry, but Scamper is too playful to be part of my collection.

Herbert Delgato

arfy,

don't be sad. you're a gooooood doggy.

thank you for trying to find me a home. i sang! i cuddled! i played! i got brushed!

but...meow do i put this? none of those people were right for me. i need a home where i can do ALL of those things.

but where could we find such a place?

scamper

DEAR BUTTERNUT NURSING HOME,

CAN YOU HELP MY KITTY?

HE LOVES MUSIC. HE LOVES TO PLAY.
HE LOVES TO TAKE NAPS IN A LAP
IN A SUNNY ROOM.

AND HE LOVES MAKING PEOPLE HAPPY.

IN FACT, I THINK HE COULD HELP <u>YOU</u>!

I HOPE YOU AGREE YOUR HOME
WOULD BE PERFECT FOR HIM.

WITH LOVE,

ARFY

P.S. mew!
← THAT'S FROM SCAMPER!

To Morris, Socrates, Edie, Moe, Lizzie,
Mr. Darcy, and of course, the real Scamper

ISBN 978-1-338-86319-2

12 11 10 9 8 7 6 5 4 3 2   22 23 24 25 26 27

Printed in the U.S.A.   76

This edition first printing, September 2022

Here's how YOU can help a homeless kitty or puppy:

VOLUNTEER at a pet adoption event.

SPAY OR NEUTER your pet so there will be fewer kitties and puppies to find homes for.

DONATE to your local shelter or a national animal advocacy group, such as:

- ♡ Alley Cat Allies (alleycat.org)
- ♡ American Society for the Prevention of Cruelty to Animals (aspca.org)
- ♡ Best Friends Animal Society (bestfriends.org)
- ♡ The Humane Society (humanesociety.org)
- ♡ Stray Pet Advocacy (straypetadvocacy.org)

ADOPT a shelter animal instead of buying a pet. **DON'T FORGET** to meet ALL the kitties and pooches. Remember, some may be shy. Some may be scared. Some are older, or tired, or even missing a leg. They need love, too, and they haven't given up! Give the "unlovables" a chance to win your heart!

LOVE, scamper & ARFY